COYOTE
and the Magic Words

to storytellers everywhere
P.R.

to my little Zoe Coyote and to the coyote in all of us
S.S.

First Edition 1 2 3 4 5 6 7 8 9 10

Library of Congress Cataloging in Publication Data
Root, Phyllis. Coyote and the magic words / by Phyllis Root; illustrated by Sandra Speidel.
p. cm. Summary: After the Maker-of-all-things uses words to create the world, she allows others to use her magic words until Coyote tries her patience with his mischief. ISBN 0-688-10308-1.—ISBN 0-688-10309-X (lib. bdg.) 1. Coyote (Legendary character)—Juvenile fiction. [1. Coyote (Legendary character)—Fiction. 2. Creation—Fiction.] I. Speidel, Sandra, ill. II. Title. PZ7.R6784Co 1994 [E]—dc20 92-3893 CIP AC

COYOTE
and the Magic Words

BY
PHYLLIS ROOT

ILLUSTRATED BY
SANDRA SPEIDEL

LOTHROP, LEE & SHEPARD BOOKS   NEW YORK

Once, my children, when the world was new, all words were magic words. For that is how the Maker-of-all-things spoke the world into being.

"Earth," she said.

And the earth hung in space, green and blue and shining.

"Sun," she said.

And the bright, burning sun climbed up one side of the heavens.

"Moon," said the Maker-of-all-things. "Stars."

And the sun tumbled down the other side of the heavens so that the moon and the stars could blaze in the blackness of the sky.

"Mountains," said the Maker-of-all-things.
And the earth cracked and heaved, and the mountains lifted up their heads.

"Rivers," she said.

And the waters leaped and danced in ribbons over the land.

"Sage," said the Maker-of-all-things. "Juniper, cedar, pine."

"Lizard," she said. "Hummingbird, hawk, jack rabbit, coyote."

One by one the Maker-of-all-things named every living thing. The earth filled with flapping, leaping, fluttering, swimming, soaring, hopping, crawling.

Us, too, she made, my children. Last of all.

And the Maker-of-all-things clapped her hands and smiled, for the world pleased her.

Then, because she was tired from all her work, the Maker-of-all-things closed her eyes and slept.

All was well in the world—for as her words had been magic words, so all words were magic words. When her creatures were hungry, they had only to say "Corn," and the corn sprouted and grew tall and heavy with ripe golden ears to feed them.

When her creatures were thirsty, they had only to say "Rain," and water fell from the sky.

When they were tired, they had only to say "Night," and the skies darkened.

When they wanted to get up, they had only to say "Day," and the bright yellow sun lit up the sky.

So everyone in the world was content.

Everyone but Coyote.

Coyote was bored with eating and drinking and sleeping and waking. There must be something more in the world to do!

So he went to a man who was growing corn and said, "Look, that woman's corn is taller than yours. You should make it rain so your corn will grow faster."

The man looked at the woman's corn. It *did* look a little bit taller than his.

"Rain," he said. And the sky darkened, and water poured down.

Then coyote ran to the woman and said, "Look, that man is making it rain. He will wash away your corn if you don't stop it."

So the woman spoke: "Sun." And the rain stopped, and the sun came out and dried the earth.

"Rain!" cried the man.

"Sun!" yelled the woman.

While they were shouting at each other, Coyote ran to a
man weaving on a loom.

"You look tired, Grandfather," Coyote said. "You work
too hard. Make it dark so you can sleep."

"I *am* tired," the man agreed. "Night," he said, and the
sun went away, and the moon and stars lit the sky.

Then Coyote ran to a woman shaping a bowl out of clay.
"Grandmother, look," he cried. "It is too dark to work.
Make it day so you can see to finish your bowl."

"Day!" the woman shouted, and the sun climbed back
into the sky.

"Night!" cried the man. "Day!" screamed the woman. "Rain!" "Sun!" "Night!" "Day!"

From one to another Coyote ran. Soon the shouting reached the ears of the Maker-of-all-things and woke her.

"QUIET!" roared the Maker-of-all-things.

Everyone stopped shouting.

"What is going on?" she asked in a voice that made the earth tremble.

And they all started talking at once.

"Coyote said my corn needed rain."

"Coyote said I needed sleep."

"Coyote said—"

"Coyote said—"

"STOP!" roared the Maker-of-all-things, and her voice made the sky shake. "Do you always do what *Coyote* tells you?"

The people hung their heads and dug their toes into the dirt. No one answered.

"Where *is* Coyote?" asked the Maker-of-all-things.

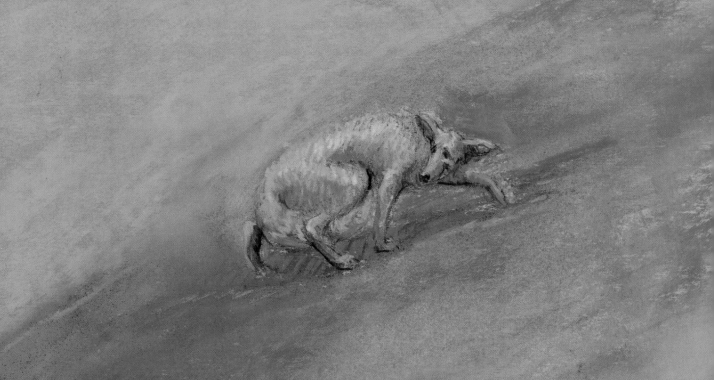

Coyote, whose laughter had stopped the moment the Maker-of-all-things had awakened, put his tail between his legs and tried to slink away. But the Maker-of-all-things saw him.

"So, Coyote," she said, "this is how you use my magic words? I will put a stop to that. From this time on, there will be no magic words.

"When you want corn, you must plant it, and tend it, and weed it, and water it.

"When you want rain, you must wait for the clouds to fill with water.

"When you are tired, you must wait until night darkens the earth, and when the sun rises you will rise, too."

"No more magic words?" said Coyote. "But think, what will the world be without magic?"

"Quieter, I hope," said the Maker-of-all-things.

"Leave us just a little magic," wheedled Coyote.

"Coyote!" thundered the Maker-of-all-things. "I think you have had quite enough magic." But she hid a smile as she said it. She knew well that Coyote hoped to make more mischief with her magic words. But she saw, too, that there was wisdom in what he said. Without magic, the world she had made would indeed be an emptier place.

The Maker-of-all-things thought for a moment. "You want my magic words, Coyote," she said. "So I will leave you this. Whenever you tell a story, your words will again be magic words. For the time of your story, magic will walk the land. But when your story is finished, the magic will be done. Now, let me get some sleep."

And the Maker-of-all-things curled up under a piñon tree and closed her eyes. The people went quietly back to their corn and their clay and their weaving, while Coyote hid in a bean patch until their anger had cooled.

And so it is, my children, that there are still magic words in the world, and I have just told you some of them. So it is, too, that Coyote goes around making up stories. He is trying to bring magic back into the world.

AFTERWORD

I FIRST MET COYOTE a few years ago when our family took a trip to the southwestern United States, where I fell in love with the desert, the sky, the colors of the rocks. In Grand Canyon National Park my daughter bought a book of coyote stories, and we read about Coyote the trickster, who sometimes out-tricks himself.

A year or so later, back home in Minnesota, I went walking on a bright and burning October day. I was thinking about stories and where they came from. And while I was thinking, Coyote appeared, to tell me that storytellers are creators. They make up worlds with their words. He didn't say it in quite that way. What he said was, "Once, my children, when the world was new, the Maker-of-all-things spoke the world into being...." So I went home and wrote down this story.

Coyote and the Magic Words shares many things with other southwestern stories, but it is not a story of any one group or tribe of people. All the plants and animals in the story are native to the southwest. Corn and beans have been grown on the land for hundreds of years. Among the Pueblo Indians, women are traditionally the potters. In some pueblos, weaving is done by men. After writing *Coyote* I discovered that there are Pueblo tales about Thinking Woman, who is a creator just as my Maker-of-all-things is a creator. As for Coyote, he has been playing tricks in stories from Guatemala to Canada for hundreds of years. In these stories Coyote is many things: a teacher, a hero, a fool, even a storyteller.

Coyote and the Magic Words is an original story. It is not a legend or a myth. It came out of my life, as all stories must. This story was given to me by a trip to the desert, a brilliant autumn day, and a wily four-legged trickster named Coyote. It was given to me to tell.

I give it to you.